For my amazingly nurturing mom and enthusiastic dad, who surrounded me with books, nature and a magical childhood where I could explore them all. For my precious children, Hattie and George, with whom I've joyously shared more piles of books, sing-alongs, impromptu dance parties, wanders through woods, laughter and wonder than I ever thought possible. And for "Bobby Downtown," my stilt-walking, roller-skating, drape-making rapper (and former '80's big hair band member) husband Trey—a dear soul who supports us all with his heart of gold.

K A C

*To my wonderful mom, who's warmth
and light will always inspire me.*

R A

The Lonely Toadstool

Text and illustration copyright © 2022 by Weave Sunshine Publishing Illustrations by Ruthie Arthur

Published in 2022 by Weave Sunshine Publishing.

Publisher's Cataloging-in-Publication data

Names: Culpepper, Kristin Addington, author. | Arthur, Ruthie, illustrator.
Title: The lonely toadstool : a children's book about emotions and new friends that come as we find our voice / by Kristin Addington Culpepper; illustrated by Ruthie Arthur.
Description: Cincinnati, OH: Weave Sunshine Publishing, 2022. | Summary: A lonely toadstool learns it is safe to use his voice and share his feelings. He's supported by diverse neighbors and new friendships form.
Identifiers: LCCN 2022901128 | ISBN: 979-8-9857772-0-8 (hardcover) | 979-8-9857772-1-5 (paperback) | 979-8-9857772-2-2 (epub) | 979-8-9857772-3-9 (kindle)
Subjects: LCSH Mushrooms--Juvenile fiction. | Emotions--Juvenile fiction. | Friendship--Juvenile fiction. | Forests and forestry--Juvenile fiction. | BISAC JUVENILE FICTION / Stories in Verse | JUVENILE FICTION / Social Themes / Emotions & Feelings | JUVENILE FICTION / Social Themes / Friendship | JUVENILE FICTION / Science & Nature / Trees & Forests
Classification: LCC PZ7.1.C838 Lon 2022 | DDC [E]--dc23

The Lonely Toadstool

by KRISTIN ADDINGTON CULPEPPER

illustrated by RUTHIE ARTHUR

One toadstool stood all alone
On the forest floor.

Surrounded by leaves beyond their prime,
He felt he wanted more.

"I'm lonesome," he said.
With that he cried
And dropped his button head.

The whimper was heard throughout the wood
And fairy and animal alike
Stopped their daily doings
To help their neighbor with his plight.

They put down their nuts and seeds,
Stopped nibbling their grass and clover,
Retired their hammers deep in the earth,
And the spinning of orbs was over.

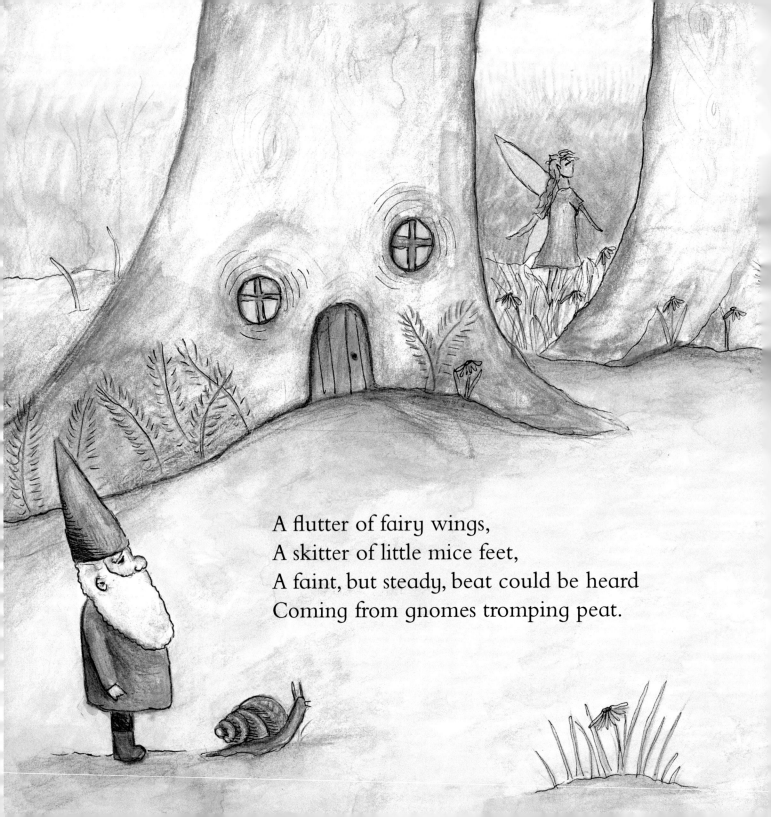

A flutter of fairy wings,
A skitter of little mice feet,
A faint, but steady, beat could be heard
Coming from gnomes tromping peat.

They bounded and they hopped,
They flew and they snuck
Out of trees, brush, dens and high nests.
They could not stop, they would not stop
Till the source of the whimper's needs was met.

"Sounds lonely,"
said one.
"Sounds sad,"
said another.
And with that,
the search party
proceeded.

The source, they did find,
Was the lonely toadstool–
They were thankful his cries they had heeded.

The sound of his neighbors caused him to lift
His tiny head up from the earth.
The love and comradery he felt at that time
Surpassed all else's worth.

They held hands and danced around him,
To show him he wasn't alone.
"But I'm NOT one of you. I'm just a toadstool,
And from here I cannot roam."

The wind, she heard his loneliness.
The rain, she heard his cry.
The sun sensed his desperation
And hid himself, with a sigh.

Now the rain could sprinkle down,
And the wind blew all around.
This continued for most of the day
In a measured and benevolent way.

His neighbors, however, remained with him,
Though they still didn't feel quite like kin.
They held him while he quietly grieved.
The lonely toadstool was still so bereaved.

Then, all of a sudden, he let out a cry,
And his despair floated away, by and by.
The wind carried it off to places unknown,
And our toadstool felt light, as though he was "home."

When just the right time finally came,
Little toadstools popped up
That looked very much the same.

There was a gasp of surprise, a giggle, then more,
As his "friends" noticed on the forest floor,
New-sprung neighbors all around—
Just like toadstool—encircling them on the ground!

So let your cries out, your anger and woe,
Along with your joys and delight.
Your neighbors will come, once they know,
And will stand with you day and night.

The sun will listen, as will the wind,
The water and wood alike.
All that can happen is wholeness
and strength when you let it all out.
It's alright.

So the lonely little toadstool,
Once alone on the forest floor,
By letting his voice and needs be heard
Found he was lonely no more.

About the Author

Kristin finds wonder and beauty in all things—her greatest inspirations being her children, love of nature and music.

Her passion for poetry had already begun by age two as she recited Mother Goose nursery rhymes and other beloved children's verses by heart. In fact, her childhood nickname was "Goose!"

Regarding *The Lonely Toadstool*, she says, "One morning I awoke with two words fresh in my mind: mushroom and poem. I followed my intuition, and later that morning *The Lonely Toadstool* came to life."

Connecting little ones and their big people with the magic of books and nature is one of her most profound joys, a natural result of the fifteen years she spent homeschooling her own children.

Kristin makes her home in Cincinnati, Ohio where she lives with her family amidst dogs, cats, fish, turtles, a herd of guinea pigs, and a mélange of furred, feathered, scaled and other forest friends.

About the Illustrator

Ruthie Arthur is an illustrator from Cincinnati, Ohio. She was graduated from Ohio University with a degree in Printmaking. She loves illustrating nature with a playful and childlike outlook.

Acknowledgements

Without Anne Stapleton's bright words of encouragement on the editing side, Susan Glassmeyer's challenges to perform my poetry "like Meryl Streep imparting her final words via Zoom to her beloved family" and Kath Grimshaw's brilliance on the design and formatting side, this baby would not be what it was meant to be. A grand "Merci," I say to you all.

Head to: ***https://www.weavesunshinepublishing.com/books-more*** for access to free bonus material to enhance your little one's experience with *The Lonely Toadstool*.

Made in the USA
Las Vegas, NV
23 October 2023

79605329R00024